a Monkey among Us

written and illustrated by
dave horowitz

HarperFestival®
A Division of HarperCollinsPublishers

A monkey.

A monkey among us.

A monkey among
a fungus.

A monkey,
humongOus.

A hippopotamus.

SPORTS

Times

HAWAII HI...

the **Hippopotamus**

SPORTS

HAWAII HIPPO...
HAVE HECK
OF A SEASON

The
Hippos had   Hawa...
there be...
ever. ...
kno...
s...

A MONKEY
...DS "FUNGUS
...MONG US"

...the first time in
...ded history a mon-
...finds not only is
...re, as he puts it, "a
...ungus among us", but
...sorces reveal he has
also proved that there
are men in bollo hats
among monkeis.
"Yeah sure they like
to say, 'there are
monkies among...

oook ooookooop
ook ooook
k ooop
ook

oooo
eep ...
he h...
eep
ooook
oooooo
he oo
ooo
ooookoo
eep eep ...
ooop eep...
oook o...
ooooook ...
eep eep ooooook oook   oooook
he he he   ...

A hippopotamus
hops a bus . . .

all
the way to
Hippotropolis.

A hippopotamus
on top of
us.

A giraffe.

Well . . .
half a
giraffe.

The
other
giraffe
half.

The bad giraffe laughs.

A monster.

A MON

A monster imposter?

It's only a monkey.

A monkey
among us.

HarperCollins®, ☷®, and HarperFestival®
are registered trademarks of HarperCollins Publishers Inc.

A Monkey Among Us
Text and illustrations copyright © 2004 by Dave Horowitz
All rights reserved. Manufactured in China.
www.harperchildrens.com

Library of Congress Cataloging-in-Publication Data
Horowitz, Dave, 1970-
A monkey among us / by Dave Horowitz.—1st ed.
p.   cm.
Summary: Illustrations and brief text follow the antics of a mischievous monkey and his animal friends.
ISBN 0-06-054335-3
[1. Monkeys—Fiction. 2. Giraffe—Fiction. 3. Hippopotamus—Fiction.] I. Title.
PZ7.H78755Mo 2004
[E]—dc21
2003008338

Typography by Joe Merkel

1 2 3 4 5 6 7 8 9 10
❖
First Edition